UNIPIGGLE
~The Unicorn Pig!~

She's a muddy
princess

He's a muddy
unicorn pig

Toge

To Meryn and all her fabulous friends

First published in the UK in 2020 by Usborne Publishing Ltd., Usborne House, 83-85 Saffron Hill, London EC1N 8RT, England. usborne.com

Text and illustrations copyright © Hannah Shaw, 2020

The right of Hannah Shaw to be identified as the author and illustrator of this work has been asserted by her in accordance with the Copyright, Designs and Patents Act, 1988.

The name Usborne and the devices 🏆 🎈 are Trade Marks of Usborne Publishing Ltd.

A CIP catalogue record for this book is available from the British Library.

ISBN 9781474972178 05660/2 FMAMJJASOND/20

Printed in UAE.

UNIPIGGLE
The Unicorn Pig!

Unicorn
Muddle

HANNAH SHAW

USBORNE

Twinkleland
Palace & gardens
Hidden cove
Better Land
The Harbour
Twinkletown
Bug Island
Village of Fancy Pants
Dragonton Cave complex
Volcano Lake

Twinkle land
★ (And surrounding kingdoms) ★

The Tree place

TwinkleSea
(Underwater Kingdom)

Twee-on-Sea

Bright point

Little Charming

Pigs Ear

The Fairy well dell
(To Rabbitland)

The Farm

Rainbow falls

The Wild bit

To other Land

THE RULES

Check: Are you smiling cheerfully?

Please remember your manners –
politeness at all times, *thank you.*

There must be no grubbiness.

Blow your nose and wash behind your ears.

Brush your hair / manes / fur / teeth.

Sit up straight.

Be neatly completely.

Best frocks (frilly dresses) and smocks (fancy tunics) only.

Hats should be worn at a jaunty 45-degree angle at all times.

Treats should be strictly rationed.

Keep fit.

Littering *is* <u>absolutely forbidden</u>, as are cobwebs, bonfires,
wasps, ants and bad smells.

No unruly parties.

If you see something wrong, put it right.

No laziness or <u>dawdling</u>.

Practice makes perfect. (Except the practice of magic.)

IMPORTANT: Do not use magic.

Magic should *not* be practised without royal permission except in a very big and terrible emergency.*

*In the event of an emergency, magic should not be silly, dangerous, ridiculous, too obvious or stinky.

Finally, be perfect.

Much obliged, their Royal Highnesses,

the <u>King and Queen</u>

100%
PERFECT

Queen Bee   *King Barry*

A copy of the Official Rule Book with more pernickety rules written by Queen Brunella Beatrix Bridget Basiletta Boss can be purchased from Twinkletown gift shop.

The Perfect Princess

Princess Peony Peachykins Primrose Pollyanna
Posh — Princess Pea for short — was rudely
woken from a rather lovely dream about her
unicorn-to-be. Her mummy, Queen Bee (whose
real name was also long and silly), had thrown
open the curtains and was now humming loudly
while doing her morning stretches.

Princess Pea wiggled down under the sheets and pretended not to hear her.

"Darling, do get up!" trilled the Queen from her downward-dog pose. "It's time for yoga. You have SUCH a busy schedule this morning AND the Unicorn Parade this afternoon."

Princess Pea poked her head out of the sheets and saw a new schedule had been pinned to her noticeboard.

SUNDAY

Princess Pea's Perfect Schedule:

Very early wake-up

Early stretchy yoga

Brush your teeth

Brush your hair

Singing lessons

Pan pipe lessons

Dance lesson (ballet)

Healthy breakfast

Indoor riding lesson

Art lesson

Swimming lesson

Change into best frilly frock for Unicorn Parade

Healthy lunch

Unicorn Parade (PLEASE don't be late)

Dinner (formal celebration banquet)

Bath

Bed

Everyone in the Royal Palace and the magical Kingdom of Twinkleland had been looking forward to the Unicorn Parade for months.

Princess Pea was the only member of the Royal Family who had learned to ride (Queen Bee secretly hated being out of control and King Barry just preferred to pootle around on his shiny golden bicycle).

The Princess currently rode a wooden unicorn. Her riding lessons had been tricky and every week she'd dismount with splinters in her bottom!

The Queen had declared that the Princess now needed a *real* unicorn and only the *best* would do. There would be a special parade, unicorns from all over the kingdom would compete to become the first ever **ROYAL UNICORN**: a *noble steed*, a *stylish mascot* and, most importantly to Princess Pea, her *loyal companion* (aka her new sidekick).

Princess Pea was very excited about getting her own unicorn. She had never actually met a *real unicorn* up close before but she had imagined the kind of fun and freedom she was going to have

with her special four-legged friend.

Princess Pea looked at her schedule again and groaned. There wasn't any time to do the things *she* wanted to do!

"Mummy, wouldn't it be nice if I could have the morning off?"

"Nonsense!" tutted the Queen. "Princesses can't be *lazy*. They are supposed to work very hard to be perfectly poised and particularly pleasing all the time. Now, jump out of bed... it's yoga o'clock!"

After leading Princess Pea through her stretches, Queen Bee went off to find her next victims: the Palace Pixies. She *loved* to boss them around.

The Royal Family was small, but Twinkleland Palace was enormous. Princess Pea thought it seemed far too big for just the King, the Queen and herself. The hundreds of rooms, turrets and corridors were kept immaculate by lots of pixies who had been hired for their impressive cleaning skills.

Every single pixie obeyed the rules without question and they never complained. They swept, polished and squeegeed day and night, even though Princess Pea had never even *been* in half of the rooms.

And it wasn't only the Palace Pixies who worked hard. Almost everyone else in the Kingdom of Twinkleland did all they could to meet the high standards expected by Queen Bee.

100% PERFECTION.

Everyone, that is, except Princess Pea.

As soon as Princess Pea was alone, she bellyflopped back onto her bed and lay there for a moment, hatching an alternative plan for the day. Then, still wearing her pyjamas, she went out to her balcony and breathed in the sweet fresh air.

It was a typical Twinkleland morning. The whole of the kingdom was bathed in golden sunlight, from the distant mountains to the nearby rooftops of Twinkletown, and she counted at least five rainbows. Drifting up from the palace garden below came the sounds of tinkling fountains, buzzing honeybees and birds crooning harmonious love songs. Just beyond the sparkling palace gates, on the far side of the turquoise moat, a herd of hopeful unicorns with shimmering coats had already arrived for the parade and were grazing in the specially-chosen Unicorn Meadow.

The trouble with living somewhere so sunshine-y was that it was nearly always too nice to stay indoors. The Princess's own plan for the day was to sneakily skip her lessons. She was sure her teachers wouldn't really mind!

Now, the Princess LIKED yoga and singing, riding practice, dancing, swimming and art. She even liked playing the pan pipes (although she preferred the drums). But she found her daily schedule a slog. **Being PERFECT was tiring**.

La La LAAA!

All the Princess's teachers were masters of their subjects, but they were utterly bamboozled by Princess Pea. She sang far too **loudly**, danced **wildly**, dive-bombed **splashily**, and her paintings were...very **splattery**!

In fact, Princess Pea's favourite lesson was gardening, mainly because she got to be outside climbing trees and digging holes and getting wonderfully muddy.

The Queen and the King despaired. "She will not listen," they moaned. "She does not obey orders and she is *always grubby*!"

So, instead of going to the Singing Room for her first lesson of the day, Princess Pea pulled on her wellies and untangled the rope ladder she kept hidden under her bed. Then she chucked it over the balcony and...escaped!

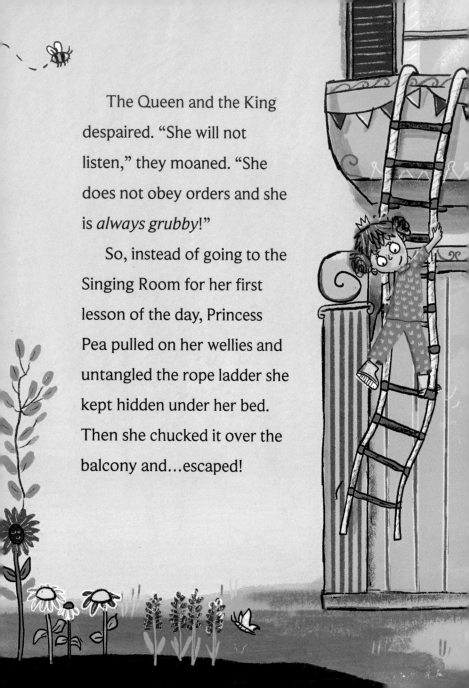

Ironing the Grass

Princess Pea landed with a **FLUMP** on the nice green grass of the First Best Palace Garden.

The gardens that surrounded the palace were quite spectacular, with something for every occasion…except a playground. There was no time in the Perfect Princess Schedule for swinging, sliding or roundabouting.

In the First Best Garden, there were lots of beautiful things…

No talking near the MUSICAL FOUNTAIN

DO NOT climb the PAGODA.

TO THE MOAT

TWINKLELAND PALACE

DO NOT TOUCH THE TOPIARY

But the princess found it *far* too snooty.

Then, the princess strolled to the

Second Best Garden…

STRICTLY NO
SPLASHING IN
THE POOL
(ICE-RINK IN
WINTER)

SIT & SMELL
THE
ROSE
GARDEN

Don't
touch

NO STOMPING
ON THE
2ND BEST
LAWN

IN

Don't get lost

OUT

NO CHEATING IN THE **MAZE**

NO POKING THE **POSH STATUES**

NO PICNICS

3rd BEST GARDEN This way

Lost in the thought of unicorns, Princess Pea nearly knocked over a pixie who had rushed up behind her.

"Eeek! Please do not walk on the grass, Princess Pea!" Arthur the Royal Gardener Pixie puffed, as he pointed to a new sign:

The palace grass must be trimmed to exactly 5 cm and kept straight at all times. All flowers must be vertical and not at all bendy. Remember, STRICTLY NO WEEDS.

"Please do not touch anything," he pleaded, looking at her big wellies. "Not *one* blade must be out of place."

"Are you ironing the grass?" laughed the Princess.

"I am!" snapped Arthur. "And what is wrong with th— Ahem, I mean, yes I am, Your Majesty!" He blushed. "*Must remember politeness at all times*," he muttered. Then he adjusted his face to a smile. "Erm…it's the Unicorn Parade today, remember, Princess!"

Princess Pea wanted to laugh again, but the poor pixie seemed so stressed. "How could I forget?" she said. "I spotted some unicorns this morning. They're in the meadow already!"

"One of those flashy fellows must have got into the gardens overnight," said Arthur, trying hard not to frown again. "They've trampled all over my tulips. Just look at those hoof prints!"

Princess Pea looked. She could see lots of little marks in the flower bed, although if they had been made by a unicorn, it must have been quite a small one.

"I'll help you put it right," she said kindly. She felt sorry for Arthur and it seemed unfair that he had to straighten an entire garden by himself, so she busied herself alongside him.

A lovely big sunflower thanked her as she propped it up with a cane. Even the flowers were polite in Twinkleland!

Thank you!

"Why don't you use a little bit of **MAGIC** to help you with the gardening?" Princess Pea asked Arthur casually.

He looked horrified. "**GASP!** We pixies would never use our magic. You know that all magic must be approved by Royal Command in Twinkleland. It's reserved strictly for emergencies, and it would definitely be *cheating* to use it for gardening." Arthur looked pleased with himself as he continued. "The Queen thinks magic is messy and unpredictable, and rightly so. You're too young to remember the Strawberry Yoghurt Flood or the Never-Ending Firework Calamity…"

The Princess had heard about these so-called disasters before — they were why the citizens of Twinkleland weren't allowed to use their magic any more. But she still couldn't understand why it was bad to have too much strawberry yoghurt or never-ending fireworks.

Arthur was still going on. "…and I shall never forget the Hubble-Bubble Enchantment, where bubbles would stream out of your ears when you thought of something funny and not one magical spell could put it right."

"Well, suit yourself," said Princess Pea. What was the point of living in a magical land where nobody practised magic? It seemed very silly to her. She couldn't wait until she was much older and able to issue Royal Commands. *Then* she'd be able to have some fun with magic!

Meanwhile, on the Parade Lawn, the Royal Tent was being erected for the Unicorn Parade. Queen Bee was cheerfully barking orders at the Tent Pixies, sending them scurrying up wobbly poles to hang bunting and flags, while she stood next to her very big flip chart, ticking things off her very long list.

Bunting ✓
Flags ✓
Seating ✓
Pink Carpet ✓
Music
Cushions
Polish the throne

Like the Princess, King Barry was also keeping a low profile. He was currently in the King's Bathroom,

grooming his prized moustache and trimming his nose hair while making up terrible, tuneless songs on his ukulele (and accidentally grooming his ukulele when he got carried away).

Princess Pea was just filling up the watering can from the charming musical fountain when

she thought she saw a flash of pink near the
big caterpillar-shaped hedge. Monsieur Tutu,
her ballet teacher, must be looking for her!
She dropped the can and ran all the way to the
Third Best Garden.

The Third Best Garden was…third-best. This was where Princess Pea was permitted to have her gardening lessons. Despite her best efforts to dig them up, there were still a number of almost-immaculate lawns with borders, a glass house and a walled salad garden (health-conscious Queen Bee had a salad obsession). Behind this, a path led to an apple orchard which grew only lovely healthy apples, not sweets. This was unusual, because elsewhere in Twinkleland, sweets grew on trees. It was here, without the knowledge of her parents or any of the pixies (except Arthur), the Princess had built herself a treehouse.

CAREFUL NOW!

ARTHUR'S SHED

APPLE ORCHARD

PRINCESS PEA'S TREEHOUSE

SALAD GARDEN

NO PICKING

Feeling confident that no one would find her in her rickety little treehouse, Princess Pea sat on her comfy old beanbag (which she'd found in the palace bins) and ate apples from the orchard. She read two fairy stories and a tatty old fact book about magical creatures that she had found exploring an attic in a forgotten turret. There were lots of exciting things in the fact book that she didn't think her parents would like…

In particular, it seemed to have an interesting, if slightly worrying, section on **UNICORNS**.

Unicorns

Horse-bodied unicorns are breathtakingly beautiful creatures with magical horns. But, beware — they are usually selfish and snooty as well as vain and boastful. They may pretend they are friendly, but in reality they are mostly concerned about themselves and their appearance. There is an old Twinkleland saying: "Hide your mirrors when a unicorn arrives."

Princess Pea was surprised. No one had told her any of this! Would her unicorn be like that? Maybe the book was out of date? She really hoped so — she had thought today was all about choosing a special friend, not a horrible snooty show-off!

Sad Salad

Ring-a-ding-ding! The bell rang for lunch. Princess Pea was *starving*. But she realized she was still wearing her pyjamas! Her schedule had said something about changing into her best frilly frock before the Unicorn Parade, so she slunk back to her room. Luckily she didn't bump into Monsieur Tutu or any of her other teachers on the way.

The Princess opened her wardrobe. It was bursting with dresses that looked like giant fluffy meringues. The Queen adored seeing her daughter in bows, ribbons, lace and ruffles. In contrast, Princess Pea hated looking like an over-iced birthday cake and there was no way she was going to wobble around in dainty shoes either.

She selected her least-worst frock and wiggled her toes in her trusty wellingtons. Surely it was only sensible to wear her wellies if she was going to be around large-hoofed animals? Happy with her reasoning, she stomped downstairs to the Grand Hall, narrowly avoiding some Stair Pixies who were scrubbing the steps clean with toothbrushes.

Toooty tooty! Parp parp!

trumpeted the Trumpet Pixie.

"Announcing the arrival of Princess Peony Peachykins for lunch," announced the Announcement Pixie.

"Princess," boomed the King happily from the very large dining table. "Let's have a cuddle!"

He looked down at Princess Pea's grubby hands as she reached him. "You smell a bit whiffy," he said to his daughter with a wrinkle of his nose. "Did you wash today?"

Princess Pea nodded. "Of course, Daddy!" she lied, mesmerized by her father's immaculately-groomed moustache. He smelled of hair wax and **EAU-DE-KING**.

"Are you excited about the Unicorn Parade?" he asked, before chattering on without pausing for an answer. "Your mummy has been *so* busy making sure everything is *absolutely perfect* as usual. She even asked the Carpet Pixies to lay out the pink carpet on the lawn. It will be like being inside but outside. Isn't that a wonderful idea?"

Princess Pea thought that a carpet might squash Arthur's superbly-ironed grass, but she didn't say anything.

TOOOTY TOOTY! PARP PARP! trumpeted the Trumpet Pixie.

"Announcing the arrival of Queen Brunella Beatrix for lunch," announced the Announcement Pixie rather hurriedly as Queen Bee rushed into the hall in her most gaudy gown, her puffy skirts billowing.

"Eat up your yummy scrummy beansprout-and-seaweed salad," the Queen said to Princess Pea as she attempted to sit down in her huge dress.

Princess Pea inspected the silver platter in front of her. It looked very *green*.

She nibbled a bit of the garnish as she watched the Serving Pixies laying out shiny cutlery and crystal goblets at the other end of the long table for the banquet later. A number of very carefully selected Twinkleland subjects had been invited to dine with the Royal Family after the Unicorn Parade. For Princess Pea it would mean sitting still and being awfully polite for longer than was comfortable, but at least there was the yummy food to look forward to.

The Princess licked her lips as she imagined huge chocolaty cakes and piles of mashed potatoes that rose higher than her tiara.

A Chef Pixie struggled in with a chalkboard. When he reached the King and Queen, he enthusiastically revealed the evening's menu with a flourish:

A SPECIAL CELEBRATION MENU FOR THE
UNICORN PARADE BANQUET

APPETIZER: Crispy Lettuce

STARTER: Boiled Beetroot with
Grated Carrot Salad

MAIN: Perfect Pickled Parsnip, Parsley
and Pumpkin Seed Platter

DESSERT: Surprise!

The Queen clapped with delight and the chef flushed with pride.

The Princess glowered. They ate salad for *every* **meal**. The fact that it was supposed to be a special day apparently made no difference.

Even though sweets grew on trees in Twinkleland, Queen Bee worried about everyone in her kingdom keeping their teeth (of all shapes and sizes) pearly white. She had banned all treats in the palace and rationed them elsewhere.

The King noticed the disappointed look on his daughter's face, so he leaned over and whispered, "Don't frown, dear. I hear we might be having *raisins* for pudding!"

"Oh…yippee," muttered Princess Pea, feeling very far from yippee indeed.

She excused herself from the long table and
went to look out of the window. The Queen
kept a pair of binoculars on the windowsill
so she could check that
everything was as it
should be outside.

Peering
through them,
Princess Pea
could see that
the palace gates
had been opened
and the unicorns
were already posing on
the pink-carpeted Parade Lawn on the far side
of the First Best Garden. Their grooms had

begun to arrive too, carrying hairdryers and
wearing utility belts loaded with brushes, combs
and hairspray, while also lugging huge boxes of
unicorn beauty products.

The Princess
sighed. She'd
been so
excited
about
having her
own unicorn,
but it seemed
like the fact book
might have been right.

A Royal Unicorn would *definitely* not want to
get muddy or dig holes or sneak into the attics

with her. And she'd been looking forward to going on adventures with her new friend outside the palace too. She felt more sinking disappointment. The day was turning out to be a disaster!

Princess Pea was just considering hiding again so she didn't have to go to the parade at all, when the Queen gave a loud shriek that made three of the Serving Pixies fall over each other.

"Oh my goodness, we have to be on the Parade Lawn in exactly ten minutes and twenty-one seconds! We must make haste!"

The Unicorn Parade

TOOTY TOOTY! PAAARP PARP!

trumpeted the Trumpet Pixie from

the edge of the Parade Lawn.

ANNOUNCING THE ARRIVAL OF THE ROYAL FAMILY.

With the King and Queen on either side,

Princess Pea was marched out onto the pink

carpet. An eager crowd had gathered, waiting

for the Unicorn Parade to start.

The Palace Pixies had followed the Royal Family from the palace in a very long neat line, and Princess Pea spotted Arthur the Gardener Pixie trailing behind at the end. His hat was bent, his shoes a little scuffed — and was that an iron burn on his smock? He looked thoroughly fed up. *Poor Arthur*, the Princess thought. She knew exactly how he felt.

Waving at Princess Pea from the crowd were a number of enthusiastic non-magical and magical creatures (who weren't allowed to use magic): pixies, fairies, trolls, mer-people, witches and wizards, and quite a few woodland animals, but no dragons as they rarely left their caves.

Some had just walked (or flown) up the hill from nearby Twinkletown, while others had travelled from far-flung parts of the kingdom, like Twee-on-Sea, Fancy Pants Village and Little Charming. They were dressed in their finest fashionable frippery, with those from Fancy Pants Village wearing their fanciest fancy pants!

Finally, Princess Pea reached the splendid Royal Tent at the end of the lawn.

The day was getting hotter and hotter, and her dress was starting to itch. She sat down on a little silver outdoor throne that had been placed on a stage and her parents sat down either side of her on their big outdoor thrones.

The King took a silver mirror out of his pocket to admire his moustache. "Oh golly, I think I forgot to trim inside this nostril!" he said, poking one finger up his nose just as the Photographer Pixie took a photo for the *Twinkleland Times*.

The Dressing-Room Tent was pitched next door, where the unicorns could be seen getting ready. Princess Pea watched them haughtily tossing their manes and whinnying shrilly while having their final brush-downs, mane-styles and massages from their personal grooms. The Princess knew that the unicorns couldn't talk, but that their grooms often understood what they were thinking.

Bleurgh! thought Princess Pea, as a waft of hairspray made her gasp for air.

"How does her young Majesty feel about choosing a Royal Unicorn?" A little fairy journalist appeared and starting asking Princess Pea questions, writing down tiny notes with  a wand-pen the size of a toothpick. "I bet everyone in the kingdom and beyond would love to be in your…er…wellies today."

Princess Pea felt rather cross and uncomfortable. She was tempted to tell the fairy

that she thought unicorns were vain, snobby
and silly, but just as she opened her mouth,
the Queen stood up to announce the
start of the parade through the gold
announcement loudspeaker.

"Welcome,
good and rule-abiding
subjects of Twinkleland. Today is an
extra-special day for us all, because one very
LUCKY unicorn will be chosen by my daughter,
Her Royal Highness Princess Pea, to become
the first, the one and only...**Royal Unicorn**.
The Royal Unicorn is to be a devoted
companion, trusty steed and henceforth the
Royal Mascot. It will be a great honour
for us to welcome the unicorn who
performs the **best** today into the
Twinkleland Royal Family."

Princess Pea snorted, while the unicorns all neighed in approval. They couldn't wait to become famous.

The Announcement Pixie took back the loudspeaker nervously and declared in a little squeaky voice: "Each unicorn will now show off their trotting skills before they treat us to a unique dance performance. The Queen will rate each unicorn in her scorebook and will consult with the Princess to help her make the final decision."

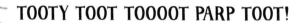

TOOTY TOOT TOOOOT PARP TOOT!

Let the UNICORN PARADE begin!

The Unicorn Surprise

As the King, Queen, Princess and the crowd watched (except for one little troll who really needed the loo), ninety-nine proud unicorns of all colours trotted up to the Royal Tent and bowed deeply. They threw their heads high and fluttered their eyelashes. Their coats dazzled and glistened and their hooves flashed.

Then, one by one, each unicorn trotted elegantly around the lawn to the sound of *Waltz of the Flowers.* The spectators clapped politely, the Queen wrote down neat notes in a very neat scorebook, and the Princess tried not to yawn too much.

Until…

All of a sudden, and quite unexpectedly, **a rather podgy, pongy and proud…PIG** was trotting past the Royal Tent. The Queen and King both gasped. The Princess started to giggle as the pig gave her an enormous wink. With his snout in the air, the pig strutted around just like the unicorns.

Princess Pea couldn't stop staring. Why was there a *pig* in the Unicorn Parade? But, wait a minute...there was something different about this pig! Was it his friendly lopsided grin? Or his grubby pink skin? And then the princess realized: *this pig had a HORN!* Wow! This was the first UNICORN PIG she'd ever seen. (It was the first anyone in Twinkleland had ever seen, for that matter.)

"GRUNT...SNORT...GRUNT."

From around the edge of the Parade Lawn came the sound of excited chatter. No one knew quite how or where the unicorn pig had come from. It hadn't been in the parade earlier. It was almost as if it had arrived by...magic.

"He looks FUN!" shouted Princess Pea.

PAUSE the parade! Summon the Rule Book Pixie!

The Rule Book Pixie
was in a flap. He
had been flicking
through the pages
of the **UNICORN
PARADE RULES**.
(It was a hefty
book — Queen Bee
had spent a whole
month coming up
with the rules and
the Writing Pixie
had obediently written
them down in super-fancy
handwriting.) But there was
nothing in it to say that pigs
weren't allowed.

"It must be a mistake!" he apologized.

The Queen laughed lightly, but Princess Pea could tell she was extremely annoyed.

"Give him a chance!" pleaded the Princess.

"Don't worry! Everyone is allowed to take part, whether horned horse or…erm…horned pig. The Princess knows how to choose the most *suitable* unicorn. Don't you, darling?"

Without giving Princess Pea time to answer, the Queen announced that because the unicorn pig was late to the proceedings, he would have to perform LAST.

Then she clicked her fingers and the music started up again.

"But I can't wait to see what he does!" protested the Princess.

"Patience is a virtue," said the Queen firmly under her breath. "Isn't it, Barry?"

The King didn't reply. Princess Pea shrugged and smiled to herself. The parade had suddenly become a lot more interesting, so she'd just have to do her best to wait.

"Barry!" hissed the Queen.

"Er, yes, dear," said the King thoughtfully.

He was twiddling his moustache and pondering why a little cloud had just appeared in the perfectly blue sky.

The Storm

Despite trying her best, Princess Pea was finding it very difficult to be patient. After the forty-ninth unicorn had performed, she began to fidget.

"This posh trotting is sooo boring!" she whispered to Arthur, who was sitting just behind her. "I can barely tell the difference between one unicorn and another. I just want to see that unicorn pig."

Arthur pretended not to hear her, as Queen Bee was sitting far too close for comfort. He stared at where the sun should have been but wasn't. Instead, big black clouds were looming ominously.

BOOOOM!

All of a sudden, a crash of thunder made everyone leap to their feet. Arthur fell off his bench, and Princess Pea jumped up with glee.

The Queen was furious. *"Pause the parade again!"* she shouted, snatching back the gold loudspeaker. *"Would the Weather Pixie consult with me urgently!"*

The unicorns had already stopped prancing and the spooked spectators stopped clapping.

Bad weather was exceedingly rare in the Kingdom of Twinkleland. The forecast was usually as perfect as everything else, which meant it was sunny at least 364 days of the year. Occasionally there was a bout of mystical fog and sometimes it snowed prettily for a day in winter, but there was only ever light drizzle to make beautiful rainbows appear.

As the worried Weather Pixie pushed his way

to the front, the uneasy crowd began to talk between themselves.

"This is most unusual!"

"And on a Sunday, what a surprise!"

With everyone distracted, Princess Pea saw a chance to stretch her legs. She slipped from her silver throne, crawled through a gap in the Royal Tent and hurried away.

As she skipped across the lawn, leaving the confusion behind her, Princess Pea's tummy rumbled. The yummy scrummy beansprouts had not been very filling. She remembered that just outside the palace gates grew a giant marshmallow tree.

At this time of year it was heavy with fluffy sweets bigger than the princess herself. There'd never been a time when the gates had been open long enough for her to sneak out and try one before. But now here she was, and no one important was watching...

"Come back, Princess," whispered the anxious daisies who grew along the palace driveway and moat-bridge.

Come back!

But the Princess decided to ignore them.
And anyway, the rain had started to fall
in great big plops from the sky and she
needed somewhere to shelter.

Meanwhile, back at the parade, the Princess was missing something extraordinary. The rain was coming down in buckets, and the wind had begun to blow as strongly and as noisily as a giant's trumpeting. The pink carpet took off like a magic carpet, and whooshed over the heads of the crowd. (It had secretly wanted to be a magic carpet all its life.) As it looped-the-loop wildly, it knocked off the King's best crown.

The crowd ran for the shelter of the Royal Tent (except for the mer-people, they were fine with getting wet). The King was finding it all very exciting indeed. He waggled his moustache energetically. "Come on in, there's plenty of room in here, come on, out of the rain!"

But the Queen was not happy about being cramped in a tent with everyone.

"Stay calm! Please don't all squash in at once!"

At first, the unicorns had been stampeding around in fury that all the attention had been taken away from them. But then their Dressing-Room Tent had flopped under the weight of the rainwater, so they were now galloping around the grass in terror, getting soaking wet and neighing with panic.

A mini tornado raged across the lawn...

The Royal Tent heaved and shook. The ropes holding it up tensed...

PING!   PING!   PING!

They broke loose from the pegs.

"Argggh!" shrieked the Queen as the tent blew away, leaving everyone running around and getting drenched.

All those feet and stampeding
unicorns quickly turned the beautiful
Parade Lawn to a muddy swamp.

And there, in the middle of the chaos,
stood the pongy, podgy unicorn pig, as cool
as a cucumber, getting splattered with mud
and loving it.

As suddenly as it started, the wind dropped, the rain stopped and the sun came out. Under a dazzling rainbow, Queen Bee found her outdoor throne and sat down.

PLUURRRP! The throne made a rude squelching noise, but the Queen managed to regally ignore it.

The pixies were already trying to rescue the Royal Tent from the rose garden and the pink carpet from the ornamental duck pond. Arthur had fetched an outdoor Hoover and was trying to suck up the muddy puddles, while the King was on his hands and knees, trying to persuade one of the stubborn palace ducks to give his best crown back.

The Queen threw her arms in the air.
"The parade must go on!" she cried.

Was anyone listening? Lots of the crowd
were already leaving. This was a disaster!

Someone had turned the music back on, but
it was playing backwards at the wrong speed
and sounded awful. The Queen was surprised to
see that only the unicorn pig carried on, happily
wiggling his bottom like nothing had happened.

The other unicorns
stared at each other
in horror.

The groom looked
alarmed. "There's no way
they can parade like this!
Look at them — they're
a mess."

They've
turned into
Muddicorns!

Indeed, the unicorns just stood there (some were stuck in the mud and couldn't move anyway). Their manes were dripping wet, their coats were plastered with muddy patches and, worst of all, they were humiliated.

"Well, Princess Pea will just have to choose one without further ado," declared the Queen. She looked around for her daughter. But all she could see was the Princess's little silver outdoor throne, upside down in the mud…

Princess? Where is my darling daughter? WHERE IS PRINCESS PEA?

The Marshmallow Rescue

The King and Queen were in a right royal panic. The Princess had disappeared!

"Maybe she blew away?" cried the King.

"My poor darling daughter," the Queen lamented. "Lost in the storm! We must get her back!" She looked towards the palace gates. Of course they were open and she knew Princess Pea a little too well.

"She went that way," chorused the ever-so-earnest daisies on the drive.

The Queen dashed out of the palace gates and over the moat-bridge, surveying the landscape, followed by the King and a small but concerned crowd.

Arthur was by the Queen's feet, hoovering up puddles before she could step in them. He stood up and looked around. "Giant marshmallows used to be on that tree," he said helpfully, pointing it out. The tree's bare branches shivered in the breeze. "The storm must have blown them off."

Queen Bee squinted. On the ground under the tree was a big pink and white flumpy mound with a single yellow muddy wellington boot sticking out of it.

"Oh GOLLY!" cried the Queen. "The Princess is trapped underneath the marshmallows!"

MMMMPPPPFFF!

came the Princess's muffled cry.

"Someone save her!" commanded the King, being the most commanding he'd ever been in his life.

The unicorns who had gathered round all looked blankly at the King. Some stuck their noses in the air and snorted moodily.

"They couldn't possibly shift all those
marshmallows, not with their dainty feet and
little horns," piped up a groom. "Especially as
everything's so *muddy* at the moment."

The Queen scanned her royal staff. But she
didn't have a special Marshmallow Clearance

Pixie, because the marshmallows had never fallen off before, and anyway, they were outside the palace grounds and the Palace Pixie work zone.

Just then, a pink blur ran past them...

WHEEE! WHEE! WHEE!

The podgy, pongy unicorn pig was squealing and running as fast as his trotters would carry him.

Mud flew in all directions as he skidded up to the pile of giant marshmallows.

"MUNCH, MUNCH, GOBBLE, SLUUUURRRP!"

The crowd watched, amazed. This was better than a Unicorn Parade!

Within minutes, the brave unicorn pig had eaten all the marshmallows (save one, which was for the Princess).

From under the sticky mess, the Princess emerged unhurt.

"You're brilliant!" said Princess Pea admiringly to the pig. "I was wondering how long it would take me to eat my way out! I've never known anyone gobble up so many marshmallows as quickly as you."

Princess Pea stood up, wiped away a blob of sweet goo from her forehead and addressed the gobsmacked crowd. "Mummy Queen! Daddy King! Good folk of Twinkleland. I have chosen my Royal Unicorn." She scratched the pig's tummy as he lay on the ground, licking his sticky chops. "He shall henceforth be named... erm, UNI...PIGGLE. Welcome to the Royal Family, UNIPIGGLE!"

As if in approval,
Unipiggle let out the
biggest burp ever.

The King smothered a laugh and the Queen elbowed him in the ribs.

"I suppose he is a very heroic pig. But surely you'd rather have a beautiful unicorn?" the Queen asked her daughter desperately.

"No, I want UNIPIGGLE," said the Princess firmly.

The unicorns whinnied in sheer disgust, kicked
their muddy hooves, turned their tails and left.

The pixies clapped politely as they didn't know
what else to do, and the daisies cheered softly.

Princess Pea hitched up her frock, climbed onto
Unipiggle's back and rode triumphantly through
the palace gates. The Unicorn Parade had been
a success after all!

A Magical Bath Time

After all the excitement of the Unicorn Parade and the storm and the marshmallows, it was decided that the Royal Banquet would be rescheduled for another day. Perfect Princesses needed their sleep.

The King and Queen were delighted that their daughter hadn't been trapped for ever under the marshmallows, even if the podgy, pongy, proud *Unipiggle* wasn't quite what they'd had in mind for Princess Pea's Royal Unicorn.

"Maybe I should write a song about Unipiggle?" said the King, as Unipiggle snuffled around exploring the Grand Hall of the palace.

"Er, not now, thanks, Daddy…" said Princess Pea, hastily moving the ukulele out of his reach. "Unipiggle is really tired, so we're off to bed."

"I have told the Stable Pixie to prepare the Royal Stables for him," said the Queen.

"But Unipiggle can't sleep in a STABLE." Princess Pea did her very best pouty face, and Unipiggle copied.

The Queen yawned. It had been a very busy day organizing something which hadn't gone to plan. She looked fondly at her difficult daughter and she couldn't muster any more bossing for now.

"Oh alright, Unipiggle can stay in your room just this once..." she relented.

"YIPPEE!" Princess Pea did a little dance and, before anyone could stop them, the Princess and her Unipiggle had galloped upstairs.

Please make sure you both have a bath first. His trotters aren't clean at all and you are decidedly sticky!

As usual, the Princess had other plans…

"We need to tiptoe past the bathroom," Princess Pea whispered to Unipiggle, "or we'll be *forced* to wash."

Unfortunately the Bath Pixies had been put on high alert for the muddy pair and spotted them both as they sneaked towards the Princess's bedroom. Unipiggle watched in confusion as Princess Pea was whisked away into a steamy room with a great deal of tutting and fussing.

The Bath Pixies approached Unipiggle with more caution, armed with pink soap, brooms and clean flannels. "Here, piggy, piggy…"

Unipiggle wasn't having any of it. He sat down and defiantly refused to move.

Meanwhile, Princess Pea was being soaked and scrubbed and… "OW!" Her hair was being untangled.

Unipiggle heard the Princess's distress and charged into the bathroom, ready once again to save his companion. He leaped into the humungous palace bath — soaking everyone and flooding the floor.

Princess Pea couldn't stop laughing as Unipiggle nudged and licked her face in concern. "Don't worry, Unipiggle, I hate baths but I'm fine!"

The pixies quickly rolled up their sleeves, dunked their brooms and began scrubbing Unipiggle all over with the perfumed pink soap while they had the chance. Princess Pea thought it was the best bath ever!

The Laundry Pixies popped in with clean pyjamas and some towels that had been folded to look like swans. The Princess's silver toothbrush and toothpaste had been laid out on a glass tray with a little note which said *Don't forget this time!*

"We have orders to come back to check you've done them," said the Bath Pixies, finally leaving the room.

Unipiggle began to relax. He lay down and farted noisily, sending bubbles to the surface of the now filthy water.

The Princess laughed. Then she thought quietly for bit…

"Unipiggle, do you have magic? Surely you must. Other unicorns have magic, even if they aren't strictly allowed to use it."

MAGIC?

Unipiggle smiled his little lopsided grin. He looked at the bar of pink soap, which was floating in a puddle on the floor. His horn began to glow a beautiful shade of luminous rainbow, then he squeezed his eyes tightly shut and took aim. The soap seemed to glow too…

"Oh!" cried the Princess. "That's cool!"

The soap stopped glowing. It was no longer pink, but instead a creamy brown colour.

The Princess leaned over the side of the bath and picked up the bar of soap to examine it. She sniffed it. It no longer smelled of roses and old ladies but of something quite scrumptious. Very carefully, she stuck out her tongue and licked it a tiny bit…

Finally she took a big bite.

"It's chocolate!" she said in awe. "You're a genius, Unipiggle!"

Unipiggle oinked happily and looked extremely pleased with himself.

Princess Pea gobbled down the rest of her delicious chocolate soap, licked her lips, and tickled her special companion behind the ear. She felt sure this was the start of some very exciting adventures with **UNIPIGGLE, the Royal Unicorn!**

Chocolate Salad

A while later, downstairs, the Queen was
relieved to get a message from the Pixie Tidy Up
Team that everything in the palace gardens was
totally spotless and back to normal. She flopped
down on her comfy, dry, indoor throne and
absent-mindedly helped herself
to what should have been
a crispy lettuce leaf from
the banqueting platter...

WHAT? Chocolate
salad?!

"Yes, I've had some of that," mumbled the King guiltily, putting down his evening newspaper. "It's delicious…but I could have sworn it was normal salad earlier! And there's something else," he continued.

"I thought that my crown was just muddy after it blew off and that duck wore it, but…"

He nibbled it.

"As I feared. Now my crown is made of chocolate too."

The Queen shook her head in disbelief.

Who on earth could have done this?

The King and Queen looked around the
Grand Hall. There wasn't a pixie in sight, the
table was clear and the floor was sparkling clean.
Except...was it?

The Queen got down on her hands and knees,
searching for clues. And then she saw it...
a muddy trotter print, just by the door...

HOW TO DRAW UNIPIGGLE

You will need: a pencil, a rubber and colouring pencils

Step 1: Draw one circle and two ovals like this...

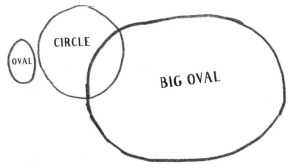

OVAL

CIRCLE

BIG OVAL

Step 2: Add the triangles for the horn, ears, legs, and draw a curly tail!

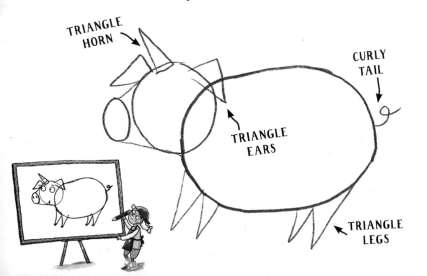

TRIANGLE
HORN

CURLY
TAIL

TRIANGLE
EARS

TRIANGLE
LEGS

Step 3: Draw in Unipiggle's face and hooves. Rub out the lines coloured purple.

FILL IN DETAILS

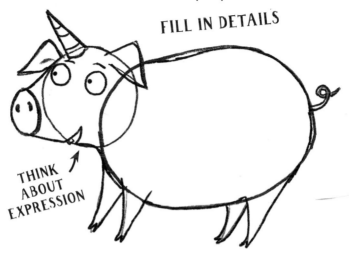

THINK
ABOUT
EXPRESSION

Step 4: Colour in Unipiggle, and TA-DAH!

ADD
SHADING
& COLOUR

& A FEW
& FLIES!

For more UNIPIGGLE activities, trot to:
www.hannahshawillustrator.co.uk

HANNAH SHAW

Hannah Shaw is a multi-award-winning author and illustrator. When she was little she wanted to be a gymnast or a champion rollerskater or a penguin keeper but instead she picked up a pen and began to draw.

Hannah now lives in Gloucestershire with her messy family. One day she hopes to meet a magical pig, but until then, she's very happy bringing UNIPIGGLE to life with her words and pictures.

Find out more about Hannah Shaw at
www.hannahshawillustrator.co.uk